Sweet Briar Goes to School

by Karma Wilson

pictures by

LeUyen Pham

DIAL BOOKS FOR YOUNG READERS

New  York

To my daughter, Christian Lorraine. When you were born, I took one look at you and declared, "Isn't she the sweetest thing?" Your papa agreed. (But every once in a while you can be a real stinker.)

—K.W.

For Caroline Kim, who could see past a skunk like me to be my friend.

—L.P.

Published by Dial Books for Young Readers
A division of Penguin Putnam Inc.
345 Hudson Street
New York, New York 10014

Designed by Kimi Weart
Text set in Plantin
Manufactured in China on acid-free paper

10 9 8 7 6 5 4 3 2 1

Library of Congress Cataloging-in-Publication Data
Wilson, Karma.
Sweet Briar goes to school / by Karma Wilson ; pictures by LeUyen Pham.
p. cm.
Summary: The other animals at school make fun of Sweet Briar because she is a skunk and has a strong smell, until she uses her scent to chase away a hungry wolf.
ISBN 0-8037-2767-4
[1. Skunks—Fiction. 2. Animals—Fiction. 3. Schools—Fiction.]
I. Pham, LeUyen, ill. II. Title.
PZ7.W69656 Sw 2003
[E]—dc21 2001051300

The illustrations for this book were prepared with watercolors on Arches cold-pressed paper.

When she was born, her mama took one look at her and declared, “Isn’t she the sweetest thing!” Her papa agreed. So they named her after the sweetest thing they could think of—the sweet briar roses growing along the garden hedge.

Every night they sang this lullaby:

"Sweet Sweet Briar,
Our pretty little rose.
A breath of fresh air
Wherever she goes."

But Sweet Briar was a skunk, and she smelled like one too. And as Sweet Briar grew, so did her aroma.

On the first day of school, Mama and Papa couldn't have been prouder.

"Off you go, Little Squirt!" said Papa.

"Remember to hold your tail high," said Mama.

Sweet Briar did. With her tail straight up, she skipped all the way to school.

But when she arrived . . .

all the students ducked under their desks and screamed, “SKUNK!”

Miss Chickory flitted and fussed. “Oh my, oh my! Is that any way to greet a classmate? What’s your name, dear?”

“Sweet Briar.”

“Welcome, Sweet Briar.” Miss Chickory pointed to a desk. “Sit right there.”

Sweet Briar sat. Everyone scooted as far away as possible.

That morning, Miss Chickory asked each student to stand up and say one nice thing about somebody else in class.

Sweet Briar pointed to the groundhog in row three. “Her fur is the color of pecans. I think pecans are beautiful.”

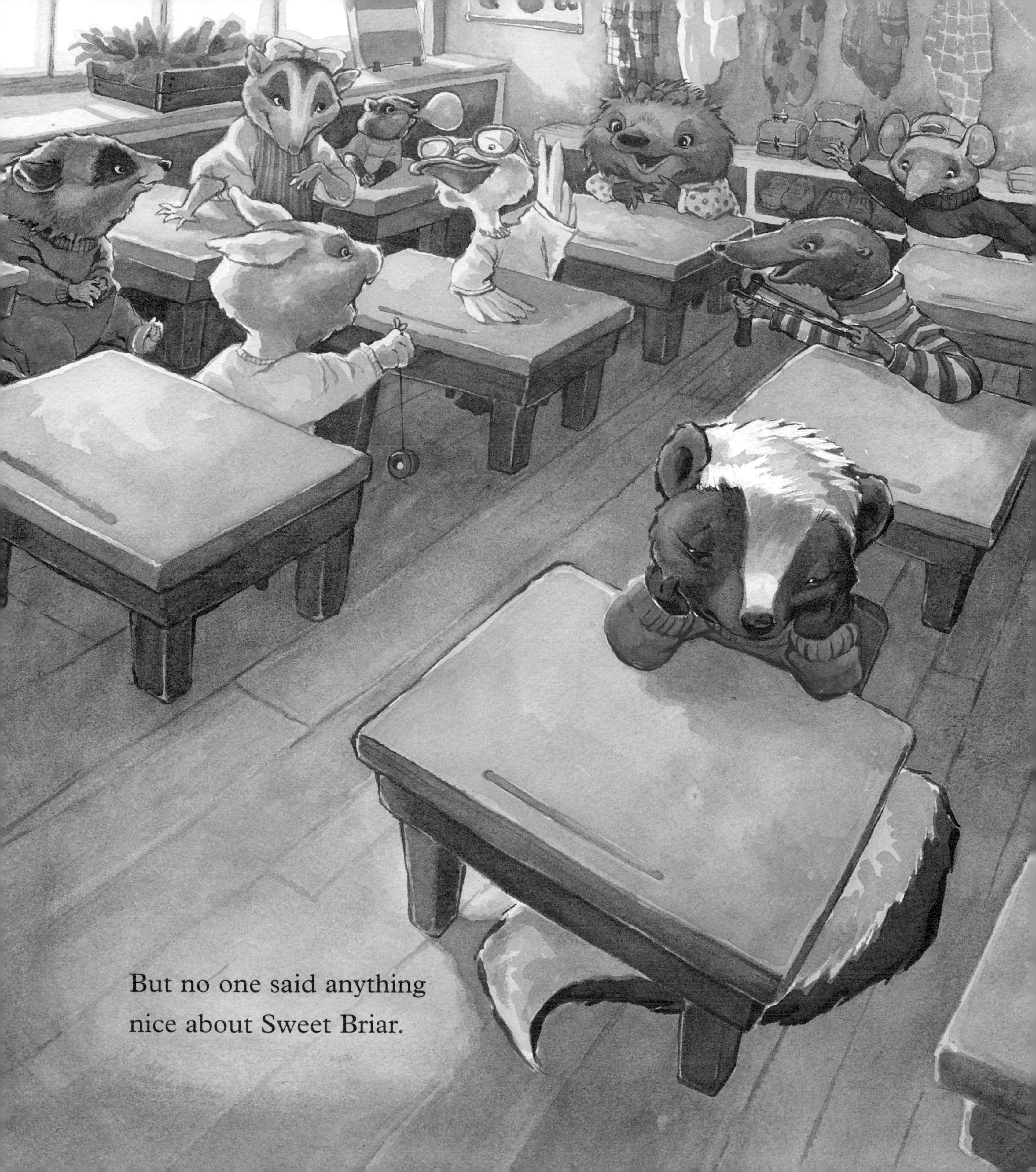

But no one said anything
nice about Sweet Briar.

To make matters worse, a lone wolf had been spotted wandering in the woods. Recess was inside.

The class played ring-around-the-rosy. Sweet Briar found herself alone, on the outside of the ring.

When Miss Chickory stepped out to clap erasers . . .

Persimmon Possum pinched her nose and said, "PEE-EEW!"

Ragweed Rat chanted, "Skunks are rotten, skunks are rotten!"

Most horrible of all, Wormwood Weasel sneered and sang:

"Stinky Sweet Briar,
She's no rose!
When she walks by,
Plug up your nose!"

After school, Sweet Briar slumped home, dragging her tail the whole way.

She didn't feel sweet. And she definitely didn't feel like a rose.

"How was school, Little Squirt?" asked Papa. Sweet Briar shrugged.

Mama frowned. "Do you feel sick?"

Sweet Briar hated for her parents to worry, so she said, "I'm fine." But she hardly ate any dinner and went to bed early.

When Mama and Papa started to sing:

"Sweet Sweet Briar,
Our pretty little—"

Sweet Briar sighed. "Not tonight please."

The next day at school, everyone showed up with paper clips on their noses.

Miss Chickory was not amused. Neither was Sweet Briar.

Later, Miss Chickory passed around letters from the alphabet. She asked each student to recite three words starting with his or her letter.

Sweet Briar got the letter *F* and said, "*F* is for *Feelings*. *F* is for *Frown*. *F* is for *Friend*."

Wormwood got the letter *S* and said, "*S* is for *Skunk*. *S* is for *Stench*. *S* is for *Smelly*." The whole class stared right at Sweet Briar.

It only helped a little when Miss Chickory said, "*S* is also for *Sit*. Do so now, Wormwood."

Once more, because of the wolf, they stayed inside for recess. The class played hide-and-seek. No one came looking for Sweet Briar.

When Miss Chickory stepped into the hall to chat with Mr. Clover . . .

Persimmon pointed at Sweet Briar and said, "Please, play somewhere else."

Ragweed shouted, "Skunks reek! Skunks reek!"

And Wormwood sang a new song. Most horrible of all, the whole class joined in:

"Stinky Sweet Briar,
She's no rose.
She smells worse
Than grizzly toes!"

Sweet Briar couldn't wait to go home.
"How was school?" asked Mama and Papa.
Sweet Briar shrugged and said, "Fine, I guess."

But that night when Papa pretended to be the Terrible Tickler, Sweet Briar barely even smiled.

When Mama offered to tell her favorite bedtime story, Sweet Briar said, “Maybe tomorrow.”

As Sweet Briar lay in bed, she listened to her parents talk outside her door.

"Something is very wrong," said Papa. "Is she having trouble fitting in?"

Mama sighed. "Probably. I remember how hard those first days of school were. A skunk's perfume can be slightly overbearing to others. We must talk to Miss Chickory."

"Most certainly," Papa said. "But I'm sure Sweet Briar will make friends soon. She's the sweetest thing in the whole world."

Sweet Briar whispered, "No, I'm not," and drifted off to sleep.

The next day, Sweet Briar dragged her tail the whole way to school.

She scrunched down in her desk all morning long.

Miss Chickory announced, “The wolf hasn’t been spotted today. Recess is outside!”

Everyone cheered. Everyone except Sweet Briar.

During recess, Sweet Briar offered her swing to Persimmon. Persimmon pretended not to notice.

Ragweed dropped his ball, so Sweet Briar tossed it back. Ragweed wouldn't touch it.

And nobody would teeter-totter with Sweet Briar.

Most horrible of all, Wormwood shouted, "Hey guys, I have a new Sweet Briar song. My funniest yet."

He sang:

"Stinky Sweet Briar,
She's no—

"Ow! Oh! ARGHH! HEELLP!"

A wolf snatched up Wormwood right in the middle of his song!

Everyone panicked!

Everyone except Sweet Briar, who remembered Mama's rule: *"To keep the wolves and bears away, lift your tail and spray, spray, spray!"*

That's just what Sweet Briar did!

She squirted that wolf right between the eyes.

The wolf dropped Wormwood and ran into the woods wailing, "SKUNK! I've been SKUNKED!"

"Me too . . ." Wormwood whimpered.

Miss Chickory ushered the class inside. “Wormwood, dear, would you sit by the window?” Then Miss Chickory declared, “Sweet Briar saved the day! There’s no need to worry about wolves with her around. We’ll make thank-you cards to show our appreciation!”

Everyone did. And *every* card said something wonderful.

Persimmon's card said:

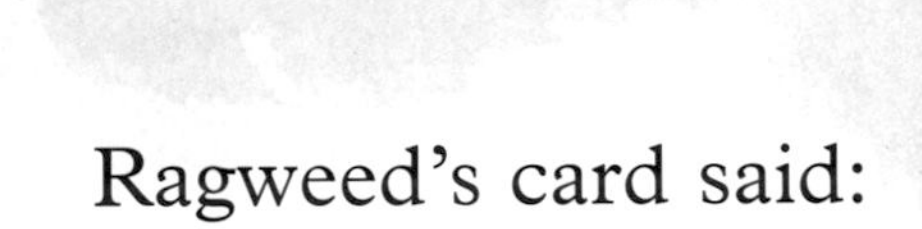

Ragweed's card said:

Wormwood's said:

Then Miss Chickory presented Sweet Briar with a special gift. "A wreath made of sweet briar roses."

A lovely aroma filled the room. The whole class took a deep whiff. Sweet Briar smelled like a rose! She couldn't wait to show her parents.

Very best of all, after school Wormwood sang a new song.

"Thanks to her
We're not wolf bait.
Sweet Sweet Briar,
She's just great!"

The whole class joined in . . .
and Sweet Briar held her tail high!